You do not need to read this page –
just get on with the book!

First published in 2010 in Great Britain by
Barrington Stoke Ltd
18 Walker St, Edinburgh, EH3 7LP

www.barringtonstoke.co.uk

ISBN: 978-1-84299-919-6

Printed in Great Britain by Bell & Bain Ltd

AUTHOR ID

Name: Alan Gibbons

Likes: My family, the North West of England, Manchester United, Thai red curry, the smell of new-mown grass, reading, daft dogs.

Dislikes: lying politicians, reality TV, muzak, litter, aggressive drivers, greedy bankers, racism, the smell of burning plastic.

3 words that best describe me: loyal, intense, passionate.

A secret not many people know: I once shook hands with the Dulux dog.

ILLUSTRATOR ID

Name: Dylan Gibson

Likes: Going out, walks, cycling, reading.

Dislikes: Sundays and Monday mornings!

3 words that best describe me: Tall, talkative and hard-working.

A secret not many people know: I hate flying!

The Dying Photo and The Book Factor

The Book Factor was a competition for school kids in Liverpool. We asked them to come up with ideas for a story they wanted to read – and we'd get a great writer to turn the winning idea into a book. Then we set up another competition to come up with ideas for the cover – and we promised to use the winning design.

James Pybis from Our Lady and St Philomena's School had a brilliant idea for the story (and he thought of the title, too). Alan Gibbons wrote it.

Luke Gates from De La Salle Humanities College came up with the perfect cover. Dylan Gibson turned it into the amazing art on the front.

Barrington Stoke published it. And you're about to read it.

We love *The Dying Photo*, from James's idea to Luke's cover. We hope you do too.

The Book Factor was run by Barrington Stoke in partnership with Booktrust and the Alt Valley Learning Network. Find out more about the competition at the end of the book!

From Alan Gibbons

This is the first time I have ever written a story from an idea thought up by someone else. I just prayed the winning entry wouldn't be about ponies, or sloppy kisses. I don't do that kind of stuff. It was lucky for me that James Pybis' idea was as scary as hell, a classic horror thriller. When I met James he didn't just have the blurb in his head but much of the plot too. I called in to see James at his school. We talked about his ideas for ten minutes or so, and I had the whole thing formed in my mind. How cool is that?

A second bonus was that the story was based in Liverpool, where I have lived for thirty years. That meant I could include my favourite places, like the Liverpool waterfront and the little streets around the Town Hall. Once I had the plot clear in my mind and its setting, I was away. Thanks to James, the story almost wrote itself. He came up with the 'what'. I just had to deliver the 'how'.

The Dying Photo is part horror story, part thriller and most of all a song of praise to the city of Liverpool. I hope you enjoy it.

To the Children, Teachers and Librarians
of Liverpool

Contents

Chapter 1
Gone

That was the day Jimmy lost his mum and dad.

The day the man with the camera took them.

The first time Jimmy saw the man, he was walking through Liverpool One, the shopping centre. He was pointing his camera at people. He didn't take any pictures at first. He didn't go up to anybody. He didn't say a word. He just watched the Christmas shoppers through his lens.

There was something odd about him.

Creepy.

He was wearing a long, black coat down to his shoes. He had a scarf round his face and he was wearing mirror sun-glasses. Finally, he had a hat pulled over his eyes. Jimmy stared. What was it? Fancy dress? He was still watching when the man turned ... and looked right at him.

Jimmy saw himself in those mirror sun-glasses. He saw himself the way the man with the camera saw him. It made him feel very small and easy to hurt. He felt his skin crawl.

"Come on, Jimmy," Dad said. "Let's get something to eat."

"Yes, stop day-dreaming," said Mum. "What are you looking at?"

Jimmy was about to point out the photographer. But he was gone. Jimmy looked left. He looked right. But he couldn't see him. All the time they were eating, Jimmy kept looking out of the window. Somehow he knew he would see the photographer again.

It didn't happen right away. They finished shopping and went to the Pier Head for a walk. The River Mersey sparkled in the winter sunlight. Seagulls hung in the clear, blue sky. It was just a few weeks until Christmas and flakes of snow were blowing. Jimmy soon forgot about the photographer. He had better things to think about. Like presents, and time off school.

"What did you get me?" he asked.

"You know we're not going to tell you that," Mum and Dad said, with a laugh.

So Jimmy looked up at the Liver Buildings. He saw the huge, bronze Liver Birds and wondered how far they could see. He thought it would be great if they could come to life and fly away across the river.

That was when he heard a man's voice. It was the photographer.

"Would you like me to take your photo?" he asked.

He was moving towards them. His feet seemed to glide over the ground. That thing he was wearing, it wasn't a coat. It was a cloak. It fluttered like wings.

"Tell him to go away!" Jimmy said.

"Why don't you want him to take our picture?" Dad asked. "It can be our Christmas family photo."

Jimmy remembered the way he had looked in the mirror sun-glasses. So small. So easy to hurt. "Don't let him take us!" he yelled.

"Oh, don't be silly," Mum told him.

The photographer pointed the camera at them. "Look at the birdy," he said.

Just then Jimmy noticed somebody waving. He turned and stared. It was a girl his age. What did she want? He was still looking at her when the camera flashed.

After that the world went crazy. Jimmy was alone. The photographer had gone.

So had the girl.

So had his parents.

"Mum?" he said. "Dad?"

But they were nowhere to be seen. He ran to the main road. Where had they gone? They had been right there, next to him. Now they were gone. His heart began to pound.

"Where are you?" he shouted.

His eyes were stinging with tears. He ran back to where they had been standing. Then he saw something on the ground. He bent down and picked it up. In his hand he had a black and white photo, one of those old negatives. The moment he looked at the photo, his skin went cold. It showed his mum and dad.

Their eyes were wide.

Their mouths were open.

They were screaming.

Chapter 2
Your Parents Are Here

An hour later Jimmy was at the police station. He sat looking down at the table in front of him. He was so alone. The police did their best. They seemed to care. He knew they were trying to help. But what could he tell them? How do you explain that a photographer has taken your parents? It sounds crazy.

So Jimmy tried showing them the photo he'd found. There were two police officers in the room. The first was called DI John Gregg.

"See?" Jimmy said. "That's Mum and Dad. They're screaming. You can tell something bad has happened."

Gregg took the photo.

"It could be a game," he said.

Jimmy wanted to scream, just like Mum and Dad in the photo.

"It's not a game!" he yelled. "The photographer took them. I know it!"

Gregg told him to calm down. Jimmy didn't want to calm down. He needed his parents. He wanted them back. Then there was a knock on the door. A policewoman came in and said something to Gregg, and he smiled.

"It's OK," he said. "Your mum and dad are here."

Jimmy jumped up and brushed away his tears. He was so happy he started laughing. His whole body shook with joy. Slowly the door opened. He took a step forward. Then the happiness died. Two strangers walked in, a man and a woman.

"I told you it would be OK," Gregg said.

It wasn't OK.

Nothing was ever going to be OK again.

They weren't Jimmy's parents. He had never seen them before.

"What are you doing?" Jimmy cried. "This isn't my mum and dad. I don't know them."

"But we phoned your house," Gregg said. "It was the number you gave us. That's how your parents knew you were here."

"They're not my parents!" Jimmy yelled.

"But we look after you. We are your foster parents," the man said.

Jimmy stared at Gregg. "I don't know what he's talking about," he said. "I've never seen them before."

"So how do you explain this?" Gregg asked.

He showed Jimmy his lap top. There was his address. But it said he lived with Mr and Mrs Trent, his foster parents.

"It's not true!" Jimmy shouted in protest.

"Is this you?" Gregg asked, pointing at the face on the lap top screen.

"Yes," Jimmy said.

"Is this where you live?" Gregg asked.

"Well ... yes," Jimmy told him.

The policeman patted Jimmy on the arm. "Then you must go with Mr and Mrs Trent, your foster parents," he said.

Jimmy tried to argue. No one would listen. He tried kicking and shouting. Still they didn't listen. They didn't shout at him or tell him off for wasting police time – they simply didn't listen to him. It was as if he wasn't really there.

In the end he had to go with Mr and Mrs Trent. He felt sick. Nothing made sense. He left the police station and followed them to their car. He was about to get in when somebody bumped into him. He looked up.

"You!" he gasped.

It was the girl from the Pier Head, the one who had waved to him.

He tried to grab her sleeve. "You saw my parents," he said. "Tell them!"

But the girl kept on walking. Soon she was lost in the crowds.

"We've got to go after her," Jimmy begged. "Please. She knows I'm telling the truth."

Mr and Mrs Trent didn't listen. They made him get in the car. *Why don't they listen?* he wondered. *Why does no one care?* Then there she was again, the girl who waved. She stepped forward. She did something with her hands. What was she up to?

Then he understood.

She was pretending to take a photo.

Chapter 3
Crazy?

"But that's my house!" Jimmy cried when the car stopped.

Mrs Trent smiled. "It's our house," she said. "How long are you going to keep up this game?"

Why didn't she get upset? She had been called up by the police to get him from the station and she didn't care. She just smiled.

Jimmy didn't like that smile. It wasn't real. It made her look like a wax dummy.

"It's not a game!" Jimmy shouted. "What are you doing here?"

Mr Trent began to laugh. "We live here. We all do. We're your foster parents. We've been looking after you for years."

Jimmy followed Mr and Mrs Trent indoors. It was his house but it had changed. The paint on the walls was a different colour. The furniture was different. Then he saw the photos in their frames. Jimmy picked them up one by one. They showed him in his school uniform. They showed him with Mr and Mrs Trent. There were pictures of them on holiday, at school plays and at family weddings.

"This can't be happening," Jimmy said.

He had a life he knew nothing about. It was as if he had lived twice, once with his own parents and once with Mr and Mrs Trent.

It was the worst day of his life. His mum and dad had vanished. Now he had new parents. They were very nice and they seemed to be worried about him. But they were strangers. It was all a bad dream.

He asked about their life together, this other one that he knew nothing about. And that was worse, because it was exactly like his real life, but with Mr and Mrs Trent in it instead of his real parents. He asked about holidays and parties. He tried to get them to make mistakes. They never did.

Am I going crazy? he wondered. *Are they right after all? Did I make up this other life? Maybe that's why everyone is so kind. Maybe that's why they don't get angry.*

Jimmy had some supper, then he went upstairs. He sat on his bed and looked at the room. It was his room but nothing was quite right. There was a photo album on the desk. He was in all the pictures but it wasn't his life. They showed him in many different places. He didn't remember any of them. He put his face in his hands.

"I want my life back," he sobbed.

He was all on his own, lost in a strange life he knew nothing about. No one was listening to him. What if they were right and he was wrong? It hurt so much, wanting his real parents back. But what if they didn't even exist?

Jimmy rubbed the tears from his eyes. He had to do something. But where could he start? What could he do?

He sighed and started to get ready for bed. He was hanging his jacket up when he felt something in the pocket.

It was a photo negative. It showed a man and woman screaming. But this time it wasn't his parents.

Jimmy stared at their faces then turned the photo over. There was a mobile number on the back. Jimmy's heart slammed. It was real. It had happened to someone else. Someone else knew about the photographer!

He phoned the number and a girl answered.

"Hello?"

"This is Jimmy Nolan," he said. "I got the photo. You're the girl I saw, aren't you? You waved at me."

"That's right," she said. "I'm Amy. I slipped the photo in your pocket when I bumped into you. We have to meet."

Suddenly Jimmy wasn't alone. Maybe together they could find out the truth.

"Do you know the Blue Star chippy?" he asked. "It's on the corner of Stopgate Lane."

"I'll find it," Amy said.

"Cool," Jimmy said. "I'll be there at five o'clock tomorrow."

"See you there," Amy said.

Then she hung up.

Chapter 4

Amy

Jimmy got off the bus and saw Amy right away.

"Hi," he said. "We have to make this quick. I have to be home ... I mean Mr and Mrs Trent's house ... by six o'clock. I told them I was going to a friend's house for tea."

They bought fish and chips and walked to Walton Hall Park. They found a bench where they could eat them and talk. Amy told her story. It was just like his. She was living with foster parents. She had started to think she was crazy.

"But you came and found me?" Jimmy said. "You didn't give up. Why?"

"My parents vanished just like yours did," she told him. "I got scared at first. Then I got angry. Do you know why?"

Jimmy shook his head.

"The photographer took my parents on my birthday," she told him. "My *birthday*! That's why I decided to fight back. Others must have vanished. Our parents aren't the only ones."

"Do you know how he does it?" Jimmy asked.

Amy gave a shrug. "It has got something to do with the camera," she said. "The only thing he leaves behind is the negative."

"Where were you when your parents were taken?" Jimmy asked.

"The last time I saw them they were outside the Town Hall," Amy said. "One minute they were there. The next they were gone."

Jimmy thought for a few moments. "Your parents vanished outside the Town Hall," he said. "Mine went from the Pier Head. That's only a five-minute walk."

Amy nodded. "I know. Whenever I can, I go down there to look for them. I took my camera with me the last time. Look who I got in the picture."

She showed Jimmy some photos.

"It's him," Jimmy gasped. "It's the photographer!"

"That's right," Amy said. "I saw him two days ago and followed him." She grinned. "I photographed the photographer."

Jimmy looked at the pictures. One was a close-up. Now he understood why the photographer wore a scarf. His skin was badly scarred. Under the scarf, the hat and the sun-glasses, he was horribly burned.

"I wonder who he is," Jimmy said.

"I don't know," Amy said. "I tried to follow him but he turned round. I hid for a moment. When I came out, he was gone."

"Do you think he lives round there?" Jimmy asked.

Amy nodded. "He was at the Pier Head then the Town Hall. I took his photo on Dale Street. That's his hunting ground. I know it."

"But why is he doing it?" Jimmy wondered.

"I think he steals people's souls," Amy said. "He's got our parents somewhere."

"So can we get them back?" Jimmy asked.

"Maybe," Amy said. "I don't know. But we have got to try. What else can we do?"

Jimmy thought for a moment. "We can try going back to where it all began," he said. "Sooner or later we will see him again ... I hope."

"Let's meet on Saturday," Amy said. "We won't go until we find him. I photographed the photographer. Now let's hunt the hunter."

Chapter 5
Hunted

Jimmy was in for a shock. He turned the corner into his street and stopped. It was the photographer. He was waiting outside the house. The moment he saw Jimmy he took out his camera and grinned.

"Look at the birdy," he said.

Jimmy turned and ran. His feet thudded on the pavement as he ran for his life. He took a left then turned right. To his horror

the photographer was waiting for him. How did he get there so quickly?

"Look at the birdy," the photographer said again.

Jimmy twisted his head. If he looked at the camera he would be gone, like his parents. He sped away. What could he do? Where could he go? He expected to see the photographer again at any moment. That was when a car pulled up. It was Mr and Mrs Trent. Jimmy couldn't believe how pleased he was to see them.

"Jump in," Mr Trent told him. "We've just been to the shops. Did you have a good time?"

"Yes, fine," Jimmy said.

"Why were you running?" Mrs Trent asked.

"Oh, it was nothing," Jimmy said. "I just felt like it."

As the car pulled away he glanced back down the street. The photographer was standing in the middle of the road. He put the camera away then he gave Jimmy a wave. It was a promise that he would be back. Soon.

Back at the house Jimmy helped Mr and Mrs Trent to put the shopping away. Then he went up to his room and phoned Amy.

"He was here," Jimmy told her. "He came looking for me. Amy, he isn't going to stop. Be careful. It could be you next."

"You're right," Amy said. "He isn't going to stop."

She was silent for a moment.

"Amy?" Jimmy said. "Are you still there?"

"I am," Amy said. "Listen. There's only one thing we can do. We've got to get him first."

Chapter 6
Morgan Slade

Jimmy and Amy met the next Saturday morning. It was Christmas Eve.

"I've got a street map," Amy said. "I marked a few places." She had made red crosses on the page. "This is where my parents vanished. This is where yours were taken. The photographer was here when I took his picture."

Jimmy drew a circle with his finger. "That's it, then. This is where he hunts."

"It's his territory all right," Amy said. "Maybe he lives here."

"Maybe," Jimmy said. "I don't know if '*live*' is the right word. He isn't human."

Amy nodded. "I know what you mean."

"So how do we find him?" Jimmy asked.

"I looked in the phone book," Amy said. "I made a list of the camera shops near here. Let's talk to them first."

There were three. No one knew anything at the first two shops. They thought Jimmy and Amy were wasting their time. It was different at the third shop.

The owner was called Mr Fox. Jimmy showed him the negative of his parents.

"This comes from a Polaroid camera," Mr Fox said. "Polaroids were popular twenty or thirty years ago. The pictures developed in the camera. You got an instant photo."

"Do you know anyone who still has one?" Jimmy asked.

"Not really," Mr Fox said.

"The man we're looking for has a badly burned face," Amy said.

Mr Fox stared at her. "What did you say?"

"His face," Amy repeated. "It's badly burned."

"There was a man," Mr Fox said. "His name was Morgan Slade. No, it can't be."

"Why not?" Jimmy asked.

"It happened a long time ago," Mr Fox said. "I was quite young at the time. I used to see him in the street. I didn't like him one bit."

"What was he like?" Jimmy asked.

"He always wore the latest fashions," Mr Fox replied. "He used to look at himself in the shop windows all the time. Oh, he loved himself. He thought he was so good-looking."

"What happened?" Amy asked. She was excited.

"There was a fire," Mr Fox said. "It destroyed the shop. But I'm sure Morgan Slade died in the flames. Yes, he was burned alive."

"Is the shop still there?" Jimmy asked.

"I think so," Mr Fox said. "It has been closed up for years."

They soon found the shop. Mr Fox was right. The windows were boarded up. The sign was still there over the door.

Morgan Slade

Photographer

"Right," Jimmy said, "this is him. What next?"

"We wait," Amy said. "The shop is in the right part of town. He has got to come back here. I know it."

They didn't have to wait long. They were looking for a way in when they heard footsteps.

"Clever boy, Jimmy," a voice said. "And well done, Amy. You found me." He gave a growl then he said the words that chilled their blood. "Look at the birdy."

"Amy!" Jimmy warned. "Don't look at the lens!"

He was too late. There was a flash and Amy was gone. A negative fluttered to the floor. Jimmy grabbed it and fled. Tears were running down his cheeks. The photographer had taken his parents. Now he had got Amy. Jimmy was alone.

He looked at the negative. He knew what he would see.

It was Amy.

Screaming.

Chapter 7
The Shop

Jimmy sat in Church Street. He stared and stared at Amy's face in the negative.

"We should have seen him coming," he said out loud. They had been watching the street. "Why didn't we see him coming?"

Then he knew.

"He was in the shop all the time!" he said. "He still lives there."

By then it was going dark. Jimmy's mobile rang. It was Mr and Mrs Trent.

"Don't worry," he said. "I'm going for the bus now."

"See you soon," Mrs Trent said.

But Jimmy was lying. It was time to fight back. He had to stop Morgan Slade before he took anyone else.

"I'm going to get you," Jimmy promised.

He jogged back to the shop. He made his hands into fists. It was his way of trying to be brave. By the time he got there it was pitch black. He crept round the back of the shop. There was a board nailed over the door. Jimmy tugged and tugged but he couldn't get it off. Then he thought of Amy and his parents. It made him strong. He tried again, pulling as hard as he could. Suddenly it gave way.

He slipped inside the shop and looked around. The only light was a street lamp. The orange light made the room look like something out of a dream. The walls were black and everything was burned. He listened for a long time before taking another step. Morgan Slade was out.

So where is your room? Jimmy wondered.

He explored for a few minutes then he found the stairs. They creaked so badly it made his heart thump. He crept along the landing and pulled back a curtain.

"Got you!" he said.

The wall facing him was covered with photos. They all showed families. Sometimes there were two or three people. Sometimes there were four or five. Jimmy looked at the way they were dressed. Morgan Slade had been doing this for years. The last two photos showed his parents ... and Amy. Every single face was twisted into a terrified scream.

On another wall there were different pictures. They were of Morgan Slade. In the first ones he looked like a ghost. You could see right through him.

"So you did die in the fire," Jimmy said.

As he ran his fingers along the row of photos, he saw that something strange happened. Morgan Slade became more and more solid. Amy had been right. He really was stealing people's souls. When he took a photo of his victims he took their lives for himself!

Jimmy stared at every photo. They told a story. Morgan Slade had brought himself back to life. Then he took more victims to heal his scars. By the tenth photo he looked almost normal. Good-looking.

But the story didn't stop there. The scars came back again. So he took more photos. He took more victims. Once more he healed.

"But you don't get better for long, do you?" Jimmy said. "You can make yourself human, but it doesn't last long. You need more and more victims to stay that way."

Then the door slammed downstairs.

It was him.

Morgan Slade.

The photographer.

Chapter 8
Show-down

Jimmy looked around and hid behind a sofa. He kept low and held his breath.

After a few moments he saw a pair of black shoes. Morgan Slade was in the room.

The photographer went over to the mirror. Jimmy watched from his hiding place as Slade removed his hat, his glasses and his scarf. For the first time Jimmy could see his face properly. Slade hardly had a single scar. He looked at his face in the mirror.

"You're nearly there, Morgan," he said. "A few more photos and you will be your old, handsome self."

Jimmy pulled a face. Photos! He meant people's souls. And he would need many more victims to keep his face that way. Jimmy's mind began to spin. He had found Morgan Slade's lair. But what was he going to do about it?

He was still trying to think of a plan when his mobile rang.

Jimmy stared at the display in horror. It was Mr and Mrs Trent. Why hadn't he switched it off?

Morgan Slade spun round. He dragged Jimmy out with his right hand and pinned him against the wall. The breath went from his body. Morgan Slade grabbed his camera with his left hand. Jimmy tried to fight but he wasn't strong enough. Slade laughed.

"Kick all you want," he said. "You won't escape. It's over."

"Let me go!" Jimmy yelled.

"Don't be silly," Slade said with a sneer. "I'm going to send you to meet your parents." He chuckled. "Look at the birdy!"

Jimmy twisted and turned. He made it hard for Slade to hold the camera steady.

Suddenly his shirt tore in Slade's hand. Jimmy broke away and sprinted for the door. Slade was too quick. He blocked the way.

"I told you there was no way out," he said.

"Get away from me!" Jimmy screamed.

"Make me," Slade said.

He raised the camera. Jimmy's blood ran cold. He had his back to the fireplace. He turned his head to one side and glimpsed a mirror hanging on the wall. He had an idea.

"Look at the birdy," Slade said again.

Jimmy reached up and pulled the mirror from the wall. Ducking his head, he held it in front of him, just as the camera flashed.

When Jimmy put the mirror down there was no sign of Slade. But his camera was sitting on the floor and there was a photo coming out of it.

Jimmy bent down and picked it up. He peeled back the photo and smiled. It showed Slade's face.

He was screaming.

Chapter 9
What Now?

Jimmy looked at the photos pinned along the wall. There would be no more souls taken from his victims. He took down a few of the photos and put them in his pocket.

He wanted to be happy. It was impossible. He was still alone. Morgan Slade had gone. But things were no better. Now he didn't even have Amy as a friend any more. It wasn't fair.

He picked up his mobile to phone Mr and Mrs Trent to take him home.

Then he heard a voice. It couldn't be! He ran to the window and looked outside.

"Amy!" he yelled.

She was standing on the pavement waving.

"You came back!" he cried.

"You did it!" Amy said. "You beat him!"

Jimmy ran down the stairs and hugged her.

"Where were you?" Jimmy asked.

"I don't know," Amy said. "It was dark and cold. I was in a dark tunnel ... and I could hear screaming."

"But Morgan Slade is gone and you came back," Jimmy said. "What does it mean? Do you think ...?"

At that moment Amy's phone rang. Her eyes widened and tears spilled down her cheeks. It was her parents, her real ones.

"I've got to go," she said. "They want to know where I am. Oh, Jimmy, they're back!"

"Do they know what's happened?" Jimmy asked.

"It's weird," Amy said. "They don't seem to remember a thing."

She turned to go. She was about to head round the corner when Jimmy's mobile rang.

"This will be Mr and Mrs Trent," he said.

But he was praying it wasn't them. He wanted it to be his parents. Amy's dream had come true. What about his?

Then there she was, on the phone, his mum, talking to him. It really was Mum. She sounded normal, as if nothing had happened.

Standing at the corner, Amy asked a question with her eyes. Jimmy nodded. She grinned.

"Stay in touch," she called.

"Where are you?" Mum asked. "It's so late, and it's Christmas Eve. Is something wrong?"

"No," Jimmy said. "Everything is just fine."

Chapter 10
The Christmas Present

It was Boxing Day. There was a knock on the door. Jimmy's mum shouted upstairs.

"Amy's here for you," she said.

"Tell her to come up," Jimmy said.

"You said you had something to show me," Amy said.

Jimmy laid out all the photos he took from Morgan Slade's room. In ten of the photos they could see Slade. In every picture he was screaming.

"What about the other ones?" Amy asked. "You said he had pictures of my parents and the other victims."

"They are really interesting," Jimmy said. He handed them to her one by one, with a big smile on his face. Every one was blank. There wasn't anyone in them.

"So Slade never came back to life," Amy said. "He died in that fire all those years ago. Is that it?"

Jimmy nodded. "I think so."

"What about the other people who vanished?" Amy asked.

Jimmy tried to sort it out in his mind. "They have got the lives they would have had if Slade had never happened," he said. "At least I think that's how it works. Maybe I'll see Mr and Mrs Trent again one day. I bet they don't know me."

"So we changed the past?" Amy said.

"Not really," Jimmy said. "Morgan Slade tried to do that. We just put things back the way they were meant to be."

"Just think," Amy said, "nobody will ever know."

Jimmy smiled. "We will," he said. "Hey, guess what I got for Christmas?"

Amy frowned. "What?"

Jimmy pulled out a digital camera. "Look at the birdy," he said.

"Now that," Amy told him, "just isn't funny."

From blurb to book

People often ask Alan Gibbons where he gets his ideas. For *The Dying Photo* the answer is simple. He got it from a boy called James Pybis. James is one of more than 500 students from schools in Liverpool who entered a competition called 'The Book Factor' to write a blurb (the stuff on the back cover that tells you about the book). They had to write a brilliant blurb for a book they wanted to read – something that would make us want to read the book right to the very end!

Lots of the blurbs sent in were amazing and it was very hard to choose a winner. Alan Gibbons and top author Frank Cottrell Boyce worked with Barrington Stoke and Booktrust to read through all of the blurbs to see which one looked the best.

Here's James's winning blurb. (He and Alan changed a few things in the plot when they talked about it afterwards – they thought about setting the story in the present day, not in the past, and they got rid of the wedding.) James even came up with the title!

1927 outside the Liver buildings. A photographer in a cloak was at Jamie's mum's wedding. As they ran out the door the photographer took the photo. The flash blinded everyone, as their sight returned the photographer had vanished along with the couple. The only clue was a picture of the couple screaming.

This project was run and funded by Booktrust, Barrington Stoke and the Alt Valley Learning Network. They would like to thank all the people who worked so hard to make this project a success – and most of all everyone who entered The Book Factor competitions. Thanks for being a part of it! You can see more about the project, including Luke Gates' winning cover design, at:
http://www.barringtonstoke.co.uk/article.asp?aid=540

Barrington Stoke would like to thank all its readers for commenting on the manuscript before publication and in particular:

Aqib Allam
Sultan Al Zahrani
Siobhan Breen
Chloe Burns
Hannah Carey
William Cheng
Daniel Church
Sebastian De Brye
Theo De Haan
Kaitlin Duff
Michael Flanagan
Cathy Harrison
Josh McKenna
Chloe McLaughlan

William Montgomery
Heather Murphy
Cyrus Nejad
Samuel Ostrovsky
Reece Palmer
Jamie Quigley
Lakshmi Rajagopal
Marcus Shades
Domenica Smailes
Jennifer Squires
Ned Thomas
Lewis Walker
Conor Wilson

Become a Consultant!

Would you like to be a consultant? Ask your parent, carer or teacher to contact us at the email address below – we'd love to hear from them! They can also find out more by visiting our website.

schools@barringtonstoke.co.uk
www.barringtonstoke.co.uk